PUFFIN BOOKS

Justin and the Demon Drop Kick

Bernard Ashley has had a long career in the teaching profession. As a young teacher in Kent he taught children with special learning difficulties. It was from this experience that he saw the need for direct reading matter that would interest older children, so he began writing his own books. He lives in Charlton, South London (not far from the scenes of his early childhood) writing books for children of all ages, from picture books to teenage novels.

BERNARD ASHELY

JUSTIN and the DEMON DROP KICK

Illustrated by Nick Ward

PUFFIN BOOKS

PUFFIN BOOKS

Published by the Penguin Group
Penguin Books Ltd, 27 Wrights Lane, London W8 5TZ, England
Penguin Putnam Inc., 375 Hudson Street, New York,
New York 10014, USA
Penguin Books Australia Ltd, Ringwood, Victoria, Australia
Penguin Books Canada Ltd, 10 Alcorn Avenue, Toronto,
Ontario, Canada M4V 3B2
Penguin Books (NZ) Ltd, Cnr Rosedale and Airborne Roads, Albany,
Auckland, New Zealand

Penguin Books Ltd, Registered Offices: Harmondsworth,
Middlesex, England

First published by Viking 1997
Published in Puffin Books 1998
3 5 7 9 10 8 6 4 2

Text copyright © Bernard Ashley, 1997
Illustrations copyright © Nick Ward, 1997
All rights reserved

The moral right of the author and illustrator has been asserted

Set in Palatino

Made and printed in England by Clays Ltd, St Ives plc

British Library Cataloguing in Publication Data
A CIP catalogue record for this book is available from
the British Library

ISBN 0–140–38015–9

One

Football in the playground at Guy Barnett Primary School wasn't like a match on television. Never mind the Arsenal or Manchester or Charlton Athletic, where two teams run out in different tops – one side wearing "away" kits so there's no clash of colours. Never mind the school team on a Saturday morning up at the park. In the playground everyone was dressed in the same school uniform; and there wasn't just one game going on, but five or six. There were games going this way, games going that way, games going crossways and some games were one-ended, going into one goal. And never mind posts and nets, the goals were coats or lunch boxes or different coloured bricks in the wall. Yet still everyone in the

playground knew where they were
kicking and who was on their side. And
watch out any idiots who got in the way
and interfered.

Mr Anchor, the head, was mustard-hot
on football, so he allowed all these balls
flying about. But the teachers reckoned *he*
didn't have to come out here on

playground duty and risk getting a smack
of plastic in the face. So they saved their
own skins and kept down at the other end
of the playground, sorting out marbles
disputes and play fights gone wrong.
They left the footballers to look after
themselves.

Up at the busy end, Justin Perfect's

match was all Year Four. Mostly boys,
except Tanya Power, who had the
midfield sewn up and was always third
or fourth to be picked. Himself, Justin
was a striker, in every meaning of the
word. He was up front, wanting the ball
to come to his head or his feet. Or he was
whacking out at anyone who fouled him.
His mum and dad said he was his own
worst enemy, but he had a few bigger
enemies than himself. Most of the
teachers, for a start.

Right now Justin was having a good
game. It was morning play, and he'd
scored a cracking goal past Kojo
Nagatamin, and Tanya Power had run up
and given him a hug. In his mind he'd
heard the shouts from the Wembley
crowd: "Per-fect! Per-fect! Per-fect!"
Everyone out of their seats and punching
the air two-fisted like one great machine.

And there was still plenty of time to go,
with another hour's game lined up for
dinner play.

He was still celebrating his goal when a
centre came in from Darren Hurst. But
with his mind on glory and not on the
ball, all he could do was chest it weakly. It
ran loose to a hacking ruck of Year Sixes.
Their game was going across Justin's, one

team's penalty area another team's right
wing. And unluckily for him, the stray
ball made Eddie Mason lose his tackle, so
Eddie swung a kick and booted it high in
the air.

Justin said something he'd have been
clouted for at home. He could have got to
that ball if Eddie hadn't kicked it. But it
went up beyond the top-floor windows,
and came down to bounce once in the

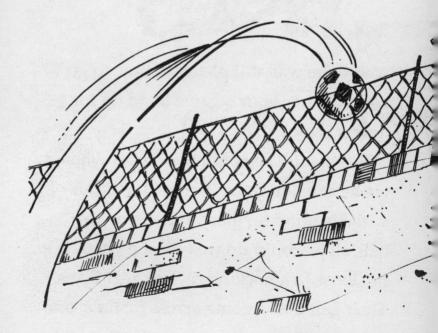

playground and then over the wall – *and* the wire mesh above it – into someone's back garden in Nigeria Road.

The next thing anyone saw was Justin, hot and angry, running down the playground and waving his arms. Not towards the wall where the ball had gone over, but down to Mrs de Sousa, on duty.

"Miss! See that? Eddie Mason kicked my ball over!"

Mrs de Sousa was Justin's class teacher. After a term of it she still lay in bed on Sunday mornings and counted the days till Justin went up into Year Five. If ever she heard the names *Justin* or *Perfect* on the *News* or in the street, she went stiff, and her teeth clenched in dread. Even a word like *just* had her ricking her neck looking round.

"Over where?" She always played for time with Justin, in case the end of the world might come first, to save her.

"Over the gardens! He done it on purpose."

"He *aimed* it?"

"He kicked it up in the air and it come down and bounced."

"Well, that's the nature of balls, Justin, to bounce. They're relied upon to do it – Wimbledon, Wembley . . ."

Justin stared at her. He couldn't scare

Mrs de Sousa the way he'd bested Mr
Cooper last year. He knew when he'd got
as far as he was going to get with her. He
said something to the tarmac and walked
back down the playground. What a
gutter! Dinner time to come, and he was
the only one in Year Four who'd brought
in a ball today. There'd be nothing to do

but try and get in someone else's game.
And for some reason no one ever wanted
him.

He walked back towards the wall as if
he were going to smack it one. But he
didn't. He stood and looked up at it. And,
giving it the eye like Mountain Rescue, he
saw where his handholds and his

footholds would be if he climbed it. The wire mesh on the top would be easy, with its neat little diamond holes to get his toes into. But he'd have to be quick, getting over before he got seen. Otherwise, it was a doddle.

Tanya came over and stared up with him. She knew what was in his mind.

"It'd be handy, that ball, at dinner time," she said. And with Tanya wanting it, that was enough for Justin.

He looked back for Mrs de Sousa. She was holding one end of a skipping rope and turning it the opposite way to the girl at the other end. Daft old bat!

Then, go!

Fingers, trainer toes and a bunk up the backside from Tanya and he was up that wall in one scramble, grabbing for the top. Another pull and his fingers would be into a wire diamond – but well in view.

He hung where he was for a second, looked round to check on Mrs de Sousa. She wasn't to be seen at the other end of the playground. Good news! Justin swung one-armed to go for the wire fence – and swung back again, quick. Because he'd seen her out of the corner of his eye. Underneath him, at the foot of the wall.

"Justin Perfect! Come down! This instant!" He had to, anyway. He couldn't

hold on. And the disgrace of it was, she had to catch him.

"You know the rule about balls gone over. Names on, and wait for them to come back."

"I weren't after a ball. I was practising an abseil."

"An abseil, Justin, is coming down."

"I was doing it the hard way."

"Walls are not for climbing. And don't shake your head!"

"But that's the nature of walls."

She'd had enough. This was just the
sort of conversation with Justin Perfect

that she repeated in her sleep. "Get up to Mr Anchor's office. Tell him I sent you, for wall-climbing and cheek."

"*Cheek?*"

"Cheek."

"I'll put my hands up to wall-climbing . . ."

"You'd have put your hands out for a dose of the cane in the good old days! Get up to Mr Anchor!"

Justin shrugged his shoulders. Wronged again. Why couldn't people believe a good lie? He started to walk like a footballer who's had a red card – a walk which took him past Eddie Mason, who was watching a long ball coming at him for a header. Justin pushed him.

"I'll get you, Mason!" he said. "Say your goodbyes!"

"*Get in!*" Mrs de Sousa screeched.

"I'm going, aren't I?" Justin said.

Two

The trouble was, Justin was on a last
chance. Three times in the Poor Behaviour
Book and you had an Order Slip. The
Order Slip went home with lines to write
and you had to bring it back signed by a
parent. And Mr Anchor had both Justin's
parents' signatures on file, for checking.
He was more careful checking Justin's
Order Slip signatures than a jeweller
taking a credit card. He would have had
fingerprint checks and forensic evidence,
if he could, because Justin's aim was to
keep school troubles at school and home
troubles at home. He no way went along
with the decision last Parents' Evening
that home and school should work
together as a team.

What it meant today – thanks to Eddie

Mason – was that one more time in the
P.B. Book would be the third (this week),
and an Order Slip would be his. And this
next Order Slip meant a hundred lines (at
school), *plus* no new bike for his birthday
(at home). It was the team against him.

He walked up the stairs to Mr Anchor's
office, which was at the top of the first
flight, at the end of the corridor – and all
quiet right now, with everyone out to
play. Justin could hear Mr Anchor talking

on the phone – it had to be the phone, because he never laughed like that with anyone in school. The door was closed – and Justin wasn't going to show himself at the arrow slit of a window. The little traffic light on the wall was amber – *I am busy, but please wait*, said the sign next to it.

Justin sighed and tried to look as if he were on some errand, in case the deputy head or Mr Branston came along. A piece of paper would help, a big piece, something as big as a sheet of marks. People didn't ask questions when you were holding a folder, or a register, or a checklist. He looked round, but there wasn't one about.

The green light would have been worst – *Come in* – whereas red would have been best – *Please see Mrs Grossmith or come back later*. With a red he could have gone away and come back later – if only his rotten memory wasn't always such a let-down.

The head's office was next to a dead end, which was a small space set out with a display: *Our School Museum*. Justin wouldn't normally give it the time of day. It wasn't up to much, as museums went. If you wanted dinosaurs you wouldn't come steaming up here. If you were after the nose cone from a space rocket or

"Torture Down the Ages" this would never be your first port of call. Old birds' nests were more likely; or the odd bit of flint and a peseta or two that Mr Anchor couldn't get changed back into British money.

But today, the museum would just give him a reason for being here. If he stood a step nearer the display there was a chance he might seem to be taking an interest in Mr Anchor's old stamp collection. *And* still be outside the head's room.

Best of all, if Mr Anchor came out, or the amber turned to green, he could almost be out of sight behind a full length display board of *People Who Help Us*.

Down in the playground the whistle

went. Soon after, lines of children were walked up the stairs by their teachers. They all turned left at the top and went along to their classrooms: Miss Goody's, Mr Branston's, Mrs Watts's. Justin stood behind the display board while they all went through, sweating in case some loudmouth gave him away. Because losing his new birthday bike would be a big and a rotten punishment for having his feet off ground, up that wall. And, a

stroke of luck, his classroom was on the
floor below, so Mrs de Sousa wouldn't be
pushing her nose round to check on him.
She wouldn't be sending for him either.
She'd never do that. She was always
saying how nice the classroom was
without him.

After the classes had gone through, it all

went very quiet. Justin could hear Mr
Anchor on the phone again, another one
of his loud laughs. He seemed happy
enough, in a good mood. It seemed a
shame to spoil it. And there had to be
some way Justin could *sort of* tell the truth
without seeming to be here in trouble. He
started to think how he might say he'd
been sent to report that his ball had gone
over, to help the caretaker. Another laugh
down the phone. On the other hand, old
Anchor was well stuck in on that chat. It
was only an hour to dinner time, if he
could keep himself out of the way. He bent
to make a proper study of the stamps of
Helvetia, wherever that was.

Which was when a woman came
slapping up the stairs in slippers, and
knocked at Mr Anchor's door. A small
woman, wearing jeans and a pink
T-shirt – and a fierce look on her face.

35

And in her arms what was she holding
but Justin's football, squashing it against
herself. It looked like something was
going to burst.

She took no notice at all of the traffic
lights. She went forward on amber,
pushed open Mr Anchor's door.

"You the 'eadmaster?"

"The headteacher, yes." Mr Anchor put down his phone just in time to catch the ball as it was flung at him.

"You can have this then. Cos I don't want it in my pond. Done for a lily, that has."

"You mean . . .?"

"What I mean is, that's come over my garden wall an' broke the stem of a lily. I'll be lucky if it hasn't sent my tadpoles berserk."

Mr Anchor wiped his wet hands on his trousers. He set the ball in his "in-tray". "I'm very sorry," he said.

"Not 'alf as sorry as me, I can tell you!"

"Is there any way . . .?" he began. Sometimes Mr Anchor tried to make things better with the school's neighbours by offering help. Community service, Year Six doing a bit of weeding, that sort of thing.

But she must have known what was
coming. "Oh no! Not your lot! Did some
work in next door's garden and had her
dead cat up. No – you just keep your balls
to yourself. Build a higher fence, or ban
'em."

"I'll put it to the governors." But she
was gone, slippers slapping again, down
the stairs.

Mr Anchor looked at the ball in his in-
tray, and at a wisp of wet weed that had
dropped on to his gold-edged invitation
to the Schools' Football Association
dinner at Wembley. He flicked off the
vegetation, picked up the ball and
inspected it. There were plenty of these
balls about, all the same design, all
supposed to be marked with the owner's

name. It was a light ball, as approved by Mr Anchor. If there were any doubt about a ball being too heavy, he would weigh it in the maths cupboard.

The ball was grazed and scarred like someone's knee, from a life of sharp bounces off bins and corners. There was a name on it – all over it – but it was faint, scuffed off, and Mr Anchor wouldn't give in to wearing glasses. He shrugged. He looked back at his wet invitation. It had to be shown on entry, and he wasn't best pleased. The wet *William Anchor* looked forged.

Stupid woman! Bringing dripping balls into his office! This was the intelligence hub of the school. Mr Anchor took it out into the corridor. He'd take this to the staffroom at the far end. Let its owner come and ask for it back, then the deputy could have a go about being more careful.

He weighed the ball in his two hands, held it in front of him like a goalie. Of course, what people like that neighbour didn't realize, he told himself, was how hard it was to keep a light ball down. Even the best player could get under a rising ball and loft it into the crowd. He stood holding the ball and looking down the long, low corridor. It took a special sort of drop kick to whack a ball thirty metres without it lifting on the way.

The corridor seemed empty. Everyone seemed busy. Mrs Grossmith's word processor was whining away, and Mrs Watts's class was chanting tables. And the empty staffroom was down at the other end, just about thirty metres – where the ball was going anyway.

From behind the museum screen Justin Perfect couldn't believe what happened next. His mouth was so far open it dried out.

Mr Anchor, headteacher, tossed the ball in front of himself, let it drop, and timed a perfect kick to send it whanging down the corridor. Low, hard, fast and straight. Just as Mr Branston, wearing his glasses, put his head out of his classroom to check the time on the corridor clock.

Three

Justin Perfect's ball caught him a smacker.
It whacked him on the side of his head
and sent his glasses flying through space.

"Yoop!" he shouted, in no known
language.

And Mr Anchor shot back into his room
like a rabbit down its hole. He grabbed up
his phone and started talking to no one,
like a lunatic. And while Mr Branston
bent for his broken glasses, saying words
which weren't in any junior dictionary,
Justin Perfect raced out of hiding and
bolted for his classroom.

Scrabbling for the pieces, Mr Branston
tried to look back through his legs. Who
could have done such an appalling thing?
There was no one in sight – not that he
could see without his glasses – but he'd

soon get to the bottom of this! He could
be a very stubborn man when he wanted.
He stuck to school rules which even the
head had forgotten. If Clive Branston
promised something, people got it, and if
he threatened something, they got that

even more. Parents asked for their children to come into his class because of his strict, firm hand. Yes, he'd have this culprit! He'd leave no stone unturned . . .

He had plenty of go in him too. He wasn't old, Mr Branston. In fact he had just got married (again), and these days he was fluffing his hair a different way, and wearing a new pair of film-star glasses.

Was wearing, because he couldn't wear them any more. Not right now. They were in two designer pieces, broken across the bridge. He weighed them in his two hands like evidence, and he stared up and down the corridor with a baffled, bathroom look. But there was no one about.

He went back into his classroom.

"Please, sir, you've broke your glasses."

"Yes." It was as if Mr Branston were
trying to weld them together with the
heat of his fingers.

"You look funny, sir."

"Yes, I expect I do."

"Like my dad before he gets up."

"Get on."

Mr Branston went back into the corridor to get the ball. In front of thirty pairs of seeing eyes he squinted at the name on it, using one half of his glasses like a magnifying glass. But he couldn't make anything out, it was still a blur.

"Can you read the name on this?" he asked Hazel Lawrence, sitting in the front.

"Yes, sir." She looked at the ball. *"Footo Scoreball."*

"They're good, them, sir," someone offered. "Don't half go."

"Not the name *of* the ball, the name *on* the ball."

"It is on the ball."

"The other name, the owner's name, the written name."

He found some patience from a reserve tank, like that mile or so before a car really does run out of petrol.

"Oh." She looked hard. "No, sir, could be . . . no. It's too faint, look . . ."

"I know it's faint, that's why I asked you. You've got young eyes."

"Eleven and a half, both of them."

"Me, sir, me, sir."

"I can read anything, sir."

"He can't, sir, I can."

Everyone started clamouring to be helpful. Well, it all took minutes off the maths.

"Leave it, leave it!" Mr Branston went over to someone he thought he could trust, pushed his face close to Mardana Kaur.

"Am I all right?" As he asked, he felt himself round the eyes, the nose, looked at his fingers for any signs of bleeding. "Am I OK?"

"Yeah, OK," Mardana told him. "A bit strict, but my mum likes that."

Mr Branston's last drop of patience was about to give out. "Mardana, stand in front of the class. If anyone misbehaves, put their name on the board."

"Yes, sir." Mardana came out, stood with arms folded like an executioner.

But while this had been going on, the ball had been left on Hazel Lawrence's table, and Leila Bloom, who sat with her,

had been giving the panels a good looking-at.

"It's Justin Perfect," she said. "This name. Look. You can see. *In* and *erf* . . ."

Mr Branston went over. He couldn't really see the autograph, but it did make sense. Justin Perfect! He was just the sort who'd do something stupid like belting a ball down the school corridor.

"Mardana!" he reminded his trusty. "Names!" And, clutching the ball and his glasses in his hands, he felt his way to the door and downstairs to Justin's classroom.

Mrs de Sousa had just got on top. She had sorted out two disputes over stickers, and a blow-up from Benjamin Ring over not being able to do the maths. She had pointed Justin Perfect to his seat when he came in, refusing to hear a word of what

he was bursting with. After all that, in came Mr Branston without his glasses and carrying a plastic football.

The class had been quiet, but for a few seconds it was a deeper, non-breathing quiet. Then the breath was let out.

"Miss, he's broke his glasses."

"Who's done that, Mr Branston?"

"It's like not having his clothes on."

"Leave it out!"

"He's taken one in the kite with that ball!"

Mrs de Sousa's class saw through to the root of things. The room was filled with pity and with great joy at the same time.

"Aaah! Bet that hurt."

"Yeah!"

But Justin had gone rigid in his seat. It

was as if his face were coated with a thin shell of ice, like a layer of make-up. If he opened his mouth to speak it would shatter and tinkle to the table in small pieces. He had never known it could be so difficult just to breathe. His back, which was sitting him up straight, felt as if spiders were rampaging up and down. Trouble caught up with Justin on a regular basis, but this was different. For a moment, he thought he might faint.

Because Justin Perfect wasn't in *this* trouble – but he knew who was. Mr William Anchor. Justin only had to say who'd sloshed Mr Branston with that ball and the school would fall down. Justin Perfect wouldn't cop it – the head would. And that was awesome.

If people believed him.

And if they didn't . . .? Justin closed his eyes, tried to breathe through his closed

mouth. He made a sound like a let-off
balloon. It would be only his word
against Mr Anchor's – and he could
picture his mum and dad asking him to
repeat his story, in the head's room. He
could see that look on his dad's face
which always showed so much sadness

and disappointment if he told a tiny little whopper.

"Do you expect me to believe that?"

"I wasn't born on a winkle barge, Justin Perfect."

It didn't look good. If Mr Anchor hadn't

owned up to Mr Branston straight off, he wasn't going to, ever. And who in the whole wide world would ever take Justin's word against Mr Anchor's?

He gripped hold of his table, tried to stop his arms from shaking. But what was this he was hearing?

"It couldn't have been Justin, Mr Branston. He was in with the head. I sent him, at playtime." That was Mrs de Sousa, fighting his corner.

Kojo was waving his arm. "Jussy's ball went over the wall, miss. Eddie Mason kicked it. Weren't Jussy for sure."

"Yes, miss. I was there."

"An' me. Spoilt our game." Good old Tanya.

There was a thin chorus of support for Justin. Which didn't quite unfreeze him yet, because he was still sitting on the cold truth. Mr Anchor had broken the

school rules – *and* Mr Branston's film-star glasses – and he wasn't owning up to it. But it helped a bit.

"Eddie Mason is more likely your culprit. He was threatened by Justin to get it back. I heard him myself." Good old Mrs de Sousa too. This could keep Justin right out of it. Now he did find breathing a bit easier. Let Eddie Mason take the bullets. If Mason got the blame, and if no one had seen Justin up in the *Our School Museum* area, then Justin wouldn't even be called as a witness. Finding life suddenly much easier, Justin wrote the right answer to a maths problem which he didn't know how to do.

"Thank you, Mrs de Sousa. Then I shall have words elsewhere." And with a look round the room for Justin, Mr Branston glared horribly at the model of a centurion, and went.

Four

Mr Branston gradually got used to the world without his glasses. At first he had gone all swimmy, but now at least he didn't think he was going to fall over. By screwing up his eyes and using one instead of two, he could just about get around without knocking into doorways.

W. ANCHOR
TOP SCORER
1953

He still couldn't tell one person from
another, but he knew he wouldn't be able
to do that till he had phoned home and
Mrs Branston had brought him his tinted
pair. However, his years of teaching had
taught him to act fast. Catch witnesses
before they forgot. Lay hold of villains
before they had time to dream up a good
story. So it was back upstairs as quickly as
he could to Eddie Mason's class.

His route took him past the head's room. He took time to go to the narrow slit of a window in the door. The red light on the indicator told him that Mr Anchor was busy, but he looked in just the same. If he could have made anything out of the blur he would have seen the headteacher being frantically busy – far too busy to be interrupted. Mr Branston went on down the corridor to 6G.

"Is Eddie Mason in here?" He threw open the door and asked the question to the noisy room. Eddie was in young Miss Goody's class, and Mr Branston didn't have to pussyfoot around being too polite to her.

"Yes, he's here, aren't you, Eddie?"

Miss Goody was young and Welsh and beautiful, and the boys in her class were in love with her, so she could get them to do things Mr Anchor and the deputy

couldn't. They were instantly quiet
whenever she said, "Six G, lips . . ." and
she put a finger to her own. And if she
said "Go there" or "Come here", they'd
do it, as if she were a princess calling
from a castle tower, and they were young
knights short of a dragon to slay.

Now she clapped her hands, as if the
sound were a spell. The class quietened.

"Oh, your poor spectacles." And with

Miss Goody saying it, no one else went
mouthing off about Mr Branston's bad
luck. She spoke beautifully for them all.
"Eddie Mason?"

Eddie sat up in his seat and nodded.
His body was straight and polite for Miss
Goody. But his face was scowling at Mr
Branston, who was holding up some ball
and screwing a mean mouth.

"This ball was kicked at me, boy!" he

said. "And I believe this is a ball you're familiar with."

"Eh?"

"You know whose this is?"

Eddie Mason looked at it. Not his. "How should I know?"

"Don't take that tone with me!"

"I don't know, do I? I haven't got a ball."

"Yes, but you know someone who has.

Someone whose ball you kicked over at playtime."

"Yeah, I know about that. That was an accident."

"Justin Perfect." Mr Branston came and bent over him. "And he threatened you as to what he'd do if you didn't get it back for him."

"Him and whose army?" Eddie looked round for the laugh.

"Has this boy been out of the room in the last ten minutes, Miss Goody?"

"He has, he asked to be excused . . . didn't you, Eddie?"

"He went to the lav, sir."

"He *was* away for rather a long time, weren't you?"

"Ah!"

"I had a pain . . ." Eddie said. He rubbed his belly to show how griped he'd been.

"Then you come with me, laddie . . ."

" 'Ang on, what am I supposed to have done? I was in the lav."

"*Not* getting a ball back in case Justin Perfect paid you out? *Not* kicking it at me in the corridor to get your own back, knowing his name was on it?"

"No, I weren't! I was in the lav, doing a sit-down." Eddie blushed. He didn't like Miss Goody being into all the private bits of his life. But it was her look which kept the class from laughing.

"Did anyone see you in there?"

"No way! It was *him* climbing up that wall. It was *him* red-hot to get his ball back. Justin Perfect, he's your man, not me!" Eddie Mason slumped in his seat. He'd been punished enough now.

"Right. Come on! Mr Anchor can go into this."

"And you'll get Justin Perfect, won't

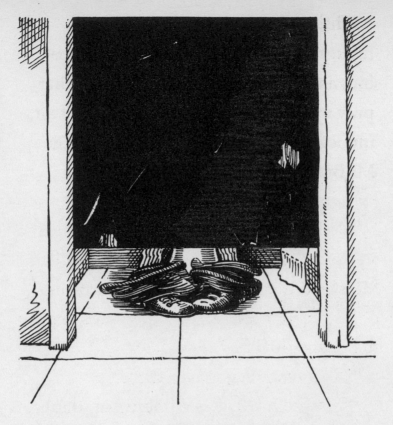

you, Mr Branston?" Miss Goody was keen
on justice being done, and on it being
seen to be done for her class.

"Of course."

"Then you go along, Eddie, and simply
tell the truth. Truth wins, doesn't it? We
know that."

Eddie got up. There was always the thought that Miss Goody might cry for him as she knelt in her nightie to say her prayers at night. And with the look of an innocent man, Eddie Mason went with Mr Branston to the head's room.

Five

Things hadn't been going so well for
Justin Perfect either. He had shown off
with a loud whoop when he got that
sum right, which had put him back into
Mrs de Sousa's mind. As a result she
had had him out and questioned him
about what Mr Anchor had said about
the wall-climbing, and the cheek.

And Justin had had to make it up,
because he could never tell the truth. He
made up how Mr Anchor had let him off

with a final warning, and how he told
him never to climb walls however much
he might want to be a mountaineer. And
then he went on to tell her about how Mr
Anchor wanted to put him in touch with
a good mountaineering club.

"So are you to go in the Poor Behaviour
Book?"

Justin had shaken his head. Which was
when Mrs Grossmith, the school
secretary, had come to get him.

The walk up the stairs to Mr Anchor's
room was like climbing the steps to the
top diving board. It was a long way up,
with a real stomach-turn to come at the
end.

Unless Mr Anchor had decided to own
up. Perhaps the secretary had said that
she'd seen Justin hanging about behind
the museum screen? Or perhaps the head
was going to offer him something to keep

his mouth shut, like a year of definitely no name going in the Poor Behaviour Book? Or a Merit Badge, or an engraved school pen for Improved Behaviour?

A shiver ran down Justin, because none

of that sounded good. He didn't like the thought of Mr Anchor down on his knees in his room, begging him not to say anything to Mr Branston. He'd rather have the punishment. Yes, by the tenth step Justin had decided he really would rather not have his mountain bike than be the boss over Mr Anchor. It was too creepy, that feeling. Justin didn't want

that power. It was better being a kid than a king.

With the traffic light at green Mrs Grossmith took Justin through into the room. And he came up short when he saw Eddie Mason in there, with Mr Branston.

Mr Anchor was sitting at his desk, the fingertips on his right hand doing a little

dance with the fingertips on his left hand. He had his *let's-be-very-fair-about-this* face on. Except the face itself was as white as that sheet of paper in front of him.

And Justin was certain now that no one knew he'd stood and watched Mr Anchor's demon drop kick from *Our School Museum*. No one knew he'd seen what he'd seen.

"Now then, Mr Branston?"

Mr Branston looked a bit puzzled – or it could have been his bare face without the glasses. But he did seem disappointed that Mr Anchor hadn't started roaring away.

Eddie Mason stood there with his eyes doing the job of a clenched fist, daring Justin to drop him in it any further.

Mr Branston folded his arms across in front of himself. "Someone, Mr Anchor, *someone* kicked a football along the middle corridor and hit me in the face with it. *Someone* broke my spectacles and almost blinded me. I'm lucky not to be in casualty, on a trolley."

Mr Anchor couldn't say a word, but he gave a grave nod and a roomful of sharp looks.

"This ball belongs to this boy." Still using one eye, Mr Branston somehow separated Justin from Eddie Mason. "But

Mrs de Sousa thinks he's innocent, and that *this* boy, Mason, went over the wall for the ball and that it was he who last held it."

Justin was a bit lost now. Who he what? But he'd never seen a headteacher look so ill, sweat so much when there weren't any big dads or mums about. And he looked older and smaller than he did in assembly or on the stairs: nothing like the man who'd scored the winner once at a Crystal Palace Reserves trial.

"Did you?" Mr Anchor asked Eddie Mason.

"No, sir, I was on the lav."

"Did *you*?" he asked Justin Perfect.

"No, sir, I was learning about another country."

"Ah. Well, two denials. Any, er, witnesses, Mr Branston?"

Mr Branston pulled a face which might

have been worth photographing for actor's courses – it had so much in it: surprise, anger, puzzlement, disappointment, self-pity. "No, no witnesses. Just . . . track record."

Mr Anchor stood up. "Ah, well, give a dog a bad name . . . on the other hand, why do dogs *get* bad names?" He glared at the boys. Off the hook now, he took his time tapping his teeth with a snapped pencil. "I shall look into this, at the

expense of my paperwork, to find the . . .
idiot . . . who'd do such a thing."

Just for a moment Justin thought Mr
Branston might cry. After all, he'd taken a
packet. A ball in the face, his glasses
broken, and no one to put the blame on.
When Mr Anchor wasn't jumping and
shouting with rage not a lot got done,
everyone knew that.

Justin suddenly made up his mind. All
at once he felt sorry for Branston. He

didn't like the man, wouldn't smile at him at the bus stop – but standing there with his face all bare, looking like someone who'd been in an accident, Justin reckoned he needed a mate.

And why should Anchor, who was starting to tidy his desk, patting a pocket as if he were feeling for one of his mints, why should he get away with it?

He ought to have owned up. Justin owned up – sometimes. His dad would own up to this. Even his cat looked ashamed if she did a mess on the carpet. So why shouldn't Anchor be a grown-up and say what he'd done, say he was sorry? He didn't have to do it with him and Eddie Mason here. He could do it on his own with Branston, and get out his wallet to pay for Branston's glasses. That's what he ought to do.

And as he thought those thoughts, a

terrible tingle came over him. A swimmy-
headed feeling that he was going to say
something. And already he could hear his
voice coming out like someone else's.

" 'Scuse me," he said. "Where's
Helvetia?"

"What?"

"Hel-who? What class is she in?" Eddie

Mason sounded as if he were going to send the boys round to give her a thumping.

"*Helvetia*. On them stamps in *Our School Museum*."

Mr Anchor looked at Mr Branston and Mr Branston tried to look at Mr Anchor.

"What are you wittering on about, boy?" The headteacher was impatient, wanted an end to all this.

"I was looking at some stamps. Didn't know where *Helvetia* was."

Mr Branston slumped at this pointless talk. But Mr Anchor was staring hard at Justin.

"Stamps?" he said. "My collection? *Out there?*"

"Yes, sir."

"*When* were you looking at them?"

"Not long back."

Mr Anchor had gone the colour

porridge goes when it's cold, with that film on it. His eyes were like two little dobs of strawberry jam put in to cheer it up.

"Up here? Out there?"

"Just after play." It was a chancy thing to say. He could suddenly catch the whole blame for this. But Justin was too far into it now – and fair was fair, all the world over.

Mr Branston grew taller. "So did you see . . .?"

"*Helvetia,*" Justin said. "I was thinking, funny name."

"It's an old-fashioned name," Mr Anchor croaked, "for Switzerland." His voice faded away into the knot of his tie.

"Don't get to the World Cup Finals a lot, do they?" Justin said. "*Haven't got the ball skills . . .*"

"If there's something you know you

should say it, boy, never mind Helvetian
ball skills . . ." Mr Branston suddenly
looked as if he could focus again. Dead
sharp, one of his eyes was.

Which was when Justin and Eddie
Mason were sent out. He and Mr
Branston would have a word, Mr Anchor
said. Things slip out of hands, people try

to hook them back, no one is above
making an error. Balls will bounce.

"It's in their nature," Justin agreed as he
went.

Mr Anchor made a noise in his throat,
something between a choke and a yodel.

Justin went back into the corridor.
Eddie hurried past him, had to go to the

lavatory again. But there was no hurry for Justin. The walk downstairs was even longer than the one coming up, and sad.

Because it would never be the same again between him and Mr Anchor. They both knew the truth of the ball business, and how the head hadn't been big enough to own up. Now he'd never look at Justin straight. And he'd give him what his dad called too much rope.

Which cast Justin down.

After all – who needed any favours from someone you wouldn't want to pick for your team?

Also in Young Puffin

I'm Trying to Tell You

Bernard Ashley

If you had a chance to talk about your school, what would you say...honestly?

Nerissa, Ray, Lyn and Prakash are all in the same class at Saffin Street School. Each of them has a story to tell about their school – sometimes dramatic, sometimes quiet, but always with a real sense of humour.

The Air-Raid Shelter

Jeremy Strong

"Girls first. You go," said Adam.
"But you're the youngest," said
Rachel.
"You're the eldest," said Adam.
They stood there and looked at each
other with set faces.

When Adam and Rachel find an old air-raid shelter they are a little scared of how dark and smelly it seems. But it is the perfect place for a secret camp and with a little work it looks quite cosy...until it is discovered by the bullying Bradley boys.

Also in Young Puffin

Rent-a-Genius

Gillian Cross

**"I know you mean well, Sophy.
But there is such a thing as being
too clever."**

Sophy Simpson loves giving people advice,
even if they don't thank her for it. She's not
going to waste any more time on her
ungrateful family – there must be somebody
out there who really needs a genius to help
them. For 50p, Sophy will tackle any
problem: from bossy grandmothers,
spots and dirty football gear to disappearing
tomatoes. The only trouble is, everyone
needs helping at once! Find out how
Sophy manages in this hilarious story.

READ MORE IN PUFFIN

For children of all ages, Puffin represents quality and variety – the very best in publishing today around the world.

For complete information about books available from Puffin – and Penguin – and how to order them, contact us at the appropriate address below. Please note that for copyright reasons the selection of books varies from country to country.

On the worldwide web: www.puffin.co.uk

In the United Kingdom: Please write to *Dept. EP, Penguin Books Ltd, Bath Road, Harmondsworth, West Drayton, Middlesex UB7 0DA*

In the United States: Please write to *Consumer Sales, Penguin USA, P.O. Box 999, Dept. 17109, Bergenfield, New Jersey 07621-0120*. VISA and MasterCard holders call 1-800-253-6476 to order Penguin titles

In Canada: Please write to *Penguin Books Canada Ltd, 10 Alcorn Avenue, Suite 300, Toronto, Ontario M4V 3B2*

In Australia: Please write to *Penguin Books Australia Ltd, P.O. Box 257, Ringwood, Victoria 3134*

In New Zealand: Please write to *Penguin Books (NZ) Ltd, Private Bag 102902, North Shore Mail Centre, Auckland 10*

In India: Please write to *Penguin Books India Pvt Ltd, 706 Eros Apartments, 56 Nehru Place, New Delhi 110 019*

In the Netherlands: Please write to *Penguin Books Netherlands bv, Postbus 3507, NL-1001 AH Amsterdam*

In Germany: Please write to *Penguin Books Deutschland GmbH, Metzlerstrasse 26, 60594 Frankfurt am Main*

In Spain: Please write to *Penguin Books S. A., Bravo Murillo 19, 1° B, 28015 Madrid*

In Italy: Please write to *Penguin Italia s.r.l., Via Felice Casati 20, I 20124 Milano*

In France: Please write to *Penguin France S. A., 17 rue Lejeune, F-31000 Toulouse*

In Japan: Please write to *Penguin Books Japan, Ishikiribashi Building, 2-5-4, Suido, Bunkyo-ku, Tokyo 112*

In South Africa: Please write to *Longman Penguin Southern Africa (Pty) Ltd, Private Bag X08, Bertsham 2013*